FREDDIE THE FROG

FREDDIE THE FROG

A STORY TOLD
BY
BROTHER DAVID

FREDDIE THE FROG

Our story begins in the spring as the snow

and ice were beginning to melt around Farmer

Brown's mill pond. Freddie showed up at the

pond on a very chilly spring day just a few years

ago. The snow was about half melted and there

weren't supposed to be any new frogs yet. The pollywog eggs had just been laid. But no matter, no matter at all, there he was, sitting on that great big rock over there in the middle of the pond. And that there rock would become his home, his throne, and his launching pad. Here he reigned and ruled over the pond.

As Freddie sat there looking around at Mr. Brown's mill pond, one of the first bugs of the season flew by the rock where Freddie was sitting. That old bug knew that he had nothing to fear, it was early in the year and he knew, he just knew, that there were no frogs around yet with long tongues and empty bellies.

But as we know, he was very wrong. One moment he was buzzing through the air, *BZZZZZZZZ*, and the next moment he was Freddie's first bug meal.

GULP------AHHHHHH!!!

And that is the way it was for many days.

All the bugs knew that it was safe to be flying

early in the spring. They all thought that there

was nothing to fear, so they helped Freddie grow

and grow **and grow**.

As spring passed and summer came,

Freddie had grown to be twice, **yes twice**,

the size of any frog that had ever lived in Mr.

Brown's mill pond, and he was still growing.

One day two bugs were flying along, not paying any attention to where they were flying. Soon there was only one bug.

When Charlie the bug realized that Freddie's long tongue had gotten his buddy Tom the bug, he took off right away for the local bug newspaper the <u>Bug Gazette</u>. There he told the bug reporters all about the big frog in the middle of the mill pond. In no time at all the <u>Bug Gazette</u> ran off a special edition called an 'extra'. The extra warned all the bugs within many miles of the mill pond to be aware of the giant frog that wanted to eat them. Every bug then knew about the giant frog of the mill pond.

Within hours it seemed that Freddie's stomach was starting to growl because there were no bugs *BZZZZZING* his way anymore. He had nothing to eat.

Freddie scanned the sky, but where ever he looked there was nothing in sight to eat, nothing at all.

Food became very, very scarce. There were those bugs that couldn't read or didn't hear about the frog, or just didn't believe. For whatever the reason, they became Freddie's only food supply and that wasn't enough for this growing frog.

Night after night Freddie would lie on his rock, thinking of some way he could get more bugs to eat. He wanted the big and juicy ones more than anything. Then, in the still of the night, a thought crossed his mind. A thought that brought a solution to his problem…

Voila, he said to himself, *I've got the answer to my dilemma.*

That night, Freddie was one happy sleeper because he had found the solution to his dilemma. In fact, he slept so relaxed you could hear his

s n o r i n g all over the pond.

As the morning sun was rising in the eastern sky, Charlie Bug and George Bug were out on an early morning cruise of the pond. They both knew about Freddie and his monster tongue, so they flew high in the air over the pond in order to stay out of range of *The Tongue* as they all called it.

As they flew overhead, Freddie launched his new "secret weapon." It was his "big green bug catcher." Suddenly Charlie was there flying next to George and the next minute he wasn't.

Freddie's new weapon had worked and he was back to filling his huge stomach.

What was Freddie's secret weapon?

What had Freddie invented?

To you and to me it is no secret weapon because we all know about it now, but never before had a frog done the "leap frog" before. Freddie was the first one to invent it and no one could do it like Freddie.

He would curl up on his rock as tight as he could. Then he would launch himself into the air. Not just a few inches like most frogs, oh no! Freddie would lift off like a rocket and head high into the air. Higher and higher he would go.

Then, when he would top off, that is, he would come to his maximum height, he would then roll over and head down. Like a green streak in the sky, he would start heading down with a lot of speed. With his mouth open and with his long tongue stretched out, he could clean the air, or as he said, "clean up." He would fill his stomach by sucking up bugs on his flight down.

Then, just before he hit the water, he would stretch out, not in a swan dive, but into what he called "the Froggie Freddie." All his legs stretched out, he hit the water like a cannon ball, throwing water everywhere.

Then he would swim over to his rock and enjoy his mouthful of lunch, or supper, or whatever.

Over the next weeks Freddie would once

again begin to grow, and grow, **and**

grow, and yes, **grow**.

It took many weeks before the bugs in the

area figured out what was happening to the

population of bugs at Mr. Brown's mill pond. By

then it was almost too late.

One day the fall leaves on the trees began to turn. That meant it was getting time for the frogs to go to the bottom of the pond and hibernate for the winter. Because it was late in the fall, each bug that Freddie now caught was a full meal in itself. They were all huge, and so was Freddie. He was the size of a small dog! Well, not really, but he was many times bigger than the other frogs.

One day Horace Frog came up on Freddie's rock and asked him if he was going to go to the bottom of the pond that night. Horace was one of the last frogs to be born that spring in the pond. That meant he was the smallest of all the frogs. Even though he was small he was quick and sometimes very fun with the jokes. He had become one of Freddie's best friends.

But when asked about going to the bottom of the pond for the winter, all Freddie could do was laugh and laugh and laugh. He told

Horace that the bugs were too big to leave. And besides, the days were still quite warm and he thought he still had plenty of time before he had to go to the bottom of the pond before the ice came.

Horace wished Freddie the best and told him he would see him in the spring. With that, he did a back flip into the water and down to the bottom he went.

Each day frog after frog would stop by the rock and urge Freddie to go with them down to the bottom of the pond and into the mud before it was too late.

And each time Freddie would laugh and laugh and laugh.

Yet, every day he knew that the time was getting shorter and shorter before the ice would come. But just as Freddie would make up his mind to go to the bottom, a warm day would come and his secret weapon would haul in the best food of the season.

One November night, Freddie couldn't take it anymore. The pond was just too cold for his blood. He was going to leave the bugs and the rock and head for the mud for the winter.

But, he said to himself, *I am going to do it in style*.

With that Freddie curled up into his Freddie launch position and then lifted off. He went higher **and higher**—higher than he had ever gone before. He went so high that the moon's rays shone on him just like a spotlight on a circus star.

Then he did the Freddie curl and headed down for the water. Faster and faster he went, closer and closer to the water he came, and then…

B A M !!!

For a few minutes Freddie laid there, half unconscious.

He thought to himself, *Wow, I must have gone straight up and come straight down right back onto my rock.*

So, Freddie did the launch curl again, and lifted off for a second try. This time we went **higher** than last time, setting a new record for height.

Then, doing the Freddie curl again, he headed down. He was nothing but a thin green streak in the full moonlit sky. Down, down, down he went. His speed increased mightily. As he got ready to hit the water, it happened…

B A M!!!

The next morning Mr. Brown walked out of the grinding mill to see the beauty of the new ice on the pond.

There, in the middle of the ice, lay-----------

YES, FREDDIE!!!

he had

DIED.

He was toooooo late.

He had waited toooooo long

to go to the bottom

of the pond.

***

A WORD FROM BROTHER DAVID

Some decisions that you put off have terrible consequences, don't they? Freddie's put-off decision cost him, well, everything, didn't it?

God is asking you to make life's most important decision without delay. Just by not making a decision, you actually have made one. Without saying 'yes' to Jesus, you are actually saying 'no' to Him.

Putting off letting Jesus come into your life will one day change where you will spend eternity after you die. If asked, Freddie would say, "See what happened to me. I waited too long."

BLESSINGS ON YOU,
Brother David